SPOTS
OR
STRIPES?

For Niru, the jungle peace keeper – V.U.

A TEMPLAR BOOK

First published in the UK in 2016 by Templar Publishing,
part of the Bonnier Publishing Group,
The Plaza, 535 King's Road, London, SW10 0SZ
www.templarco.co.uk
www.bonnierpublishing.com

First published by Penguin Random House New Zealand, 2015
Copyright © Vasanti Unka 2015

1 3 5 7 9 10 8 6 4 2

ISBN 978-1-78370-583-2 (Hardback)
ISBN 978-1-78370-584-9 (Paperback)

Printed in China

A special thank you to the World Wildlife Fund, who do a wonderful job in protecting wildlife.

SPOTS OR STRIPES?

VASANTI UNKA

t

templar publishing

Deep in the jungle,
all was at peace.

Until Tiger and Leopard
started to squabble.

The squabble turned into a quarrel.

But stripes are so **BOLD**.

Spots have

Stripes RULE

STRIPES!

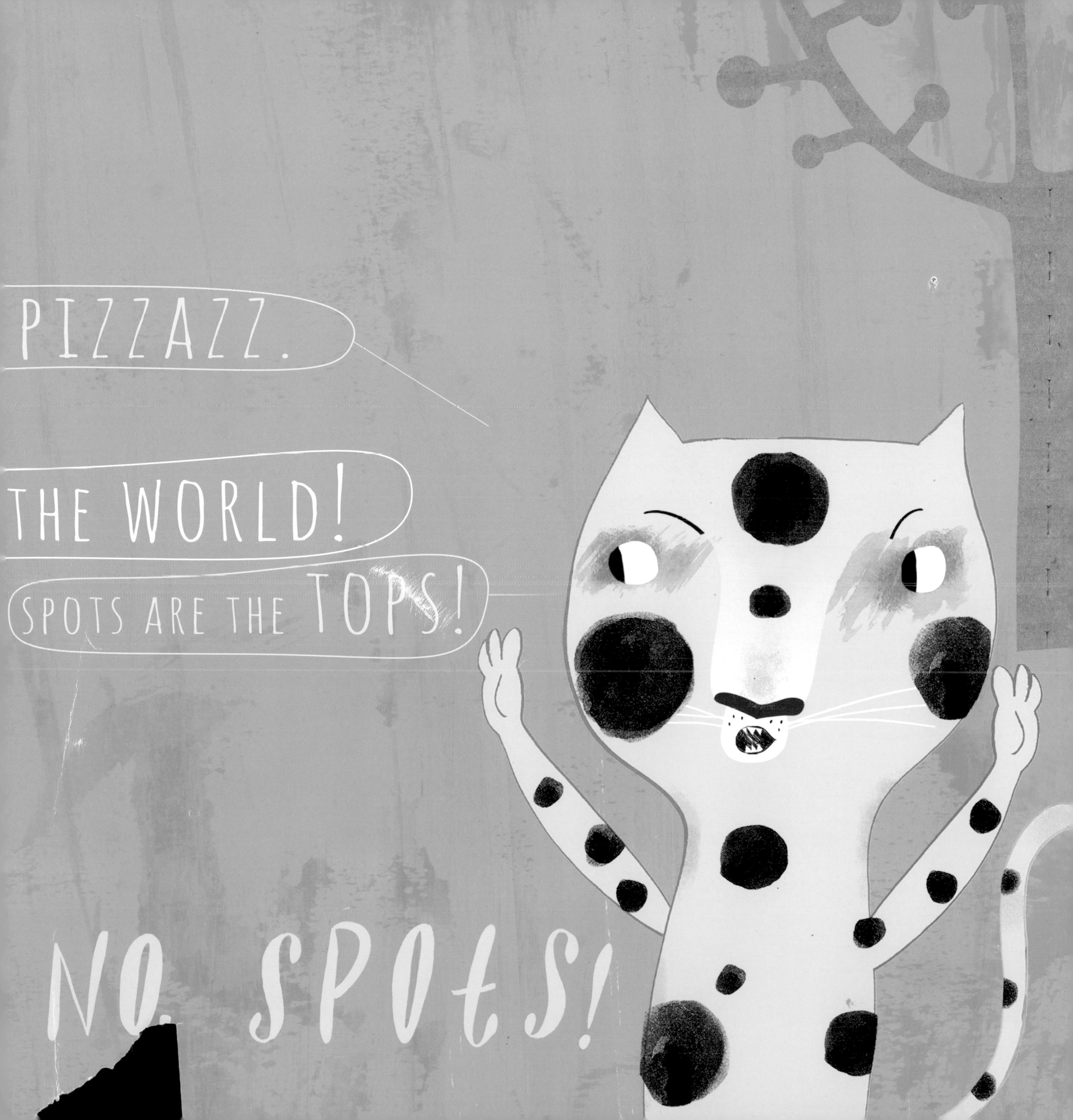
PIZZAZZ.
THE WORLD!
SPOTS ARE THE TOPS!
NO. SPOTS!

The quarrel turned into a fight.

STRIPES!

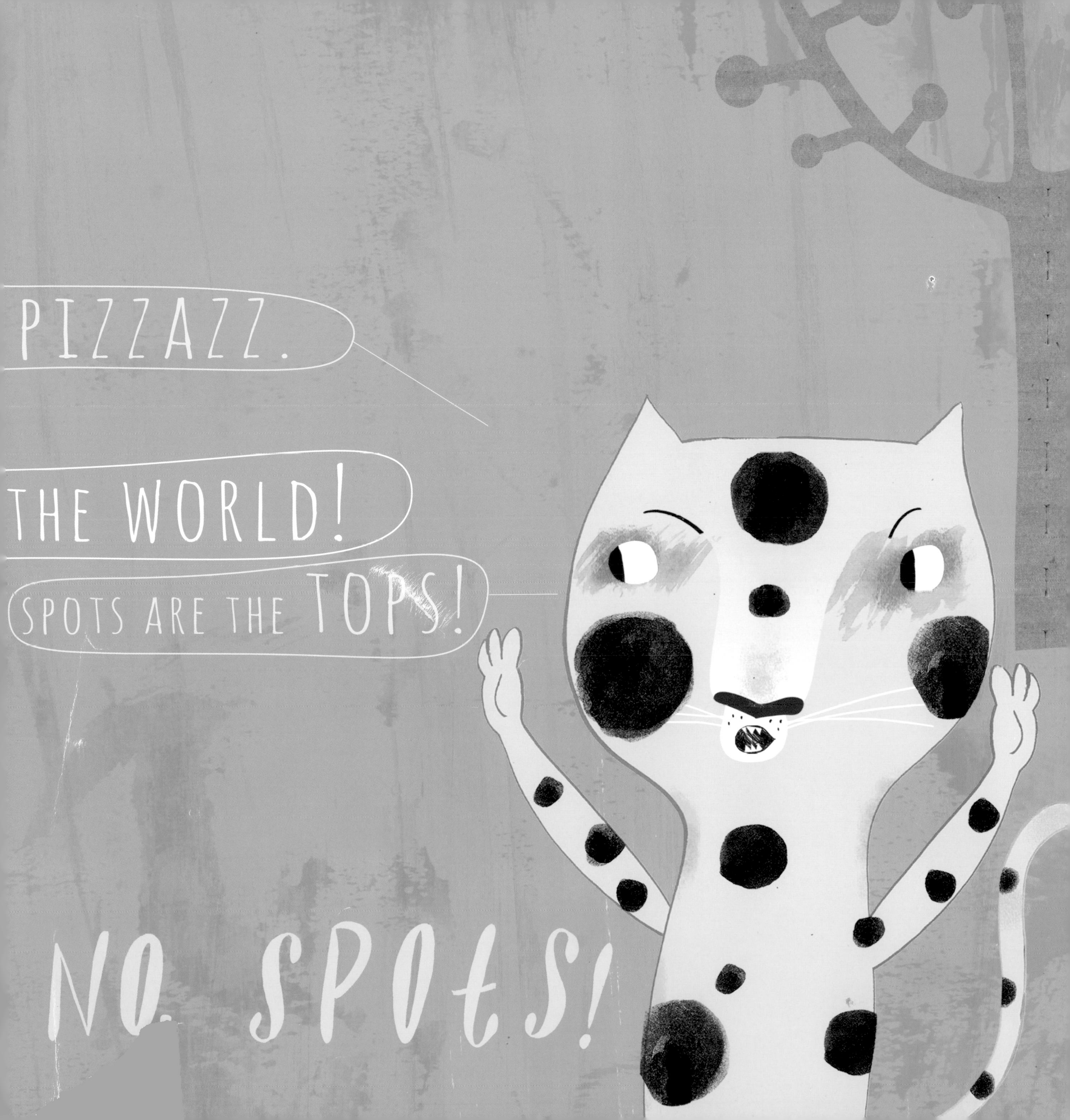
PIZZAZZ.
THE WORLD!
SPOTS ARE THE TOPS!
NO SPOTS!

The quarrel turned into a fight.

STIRTPES!

Banana-skin missiles
and mucky mud bombs
flew through the air.

By lunchtime,
the jungle was a mess.

So Monkey yelled,

CEASE

Rotten tomatoes
and smelly old eggs
exploded on trees.

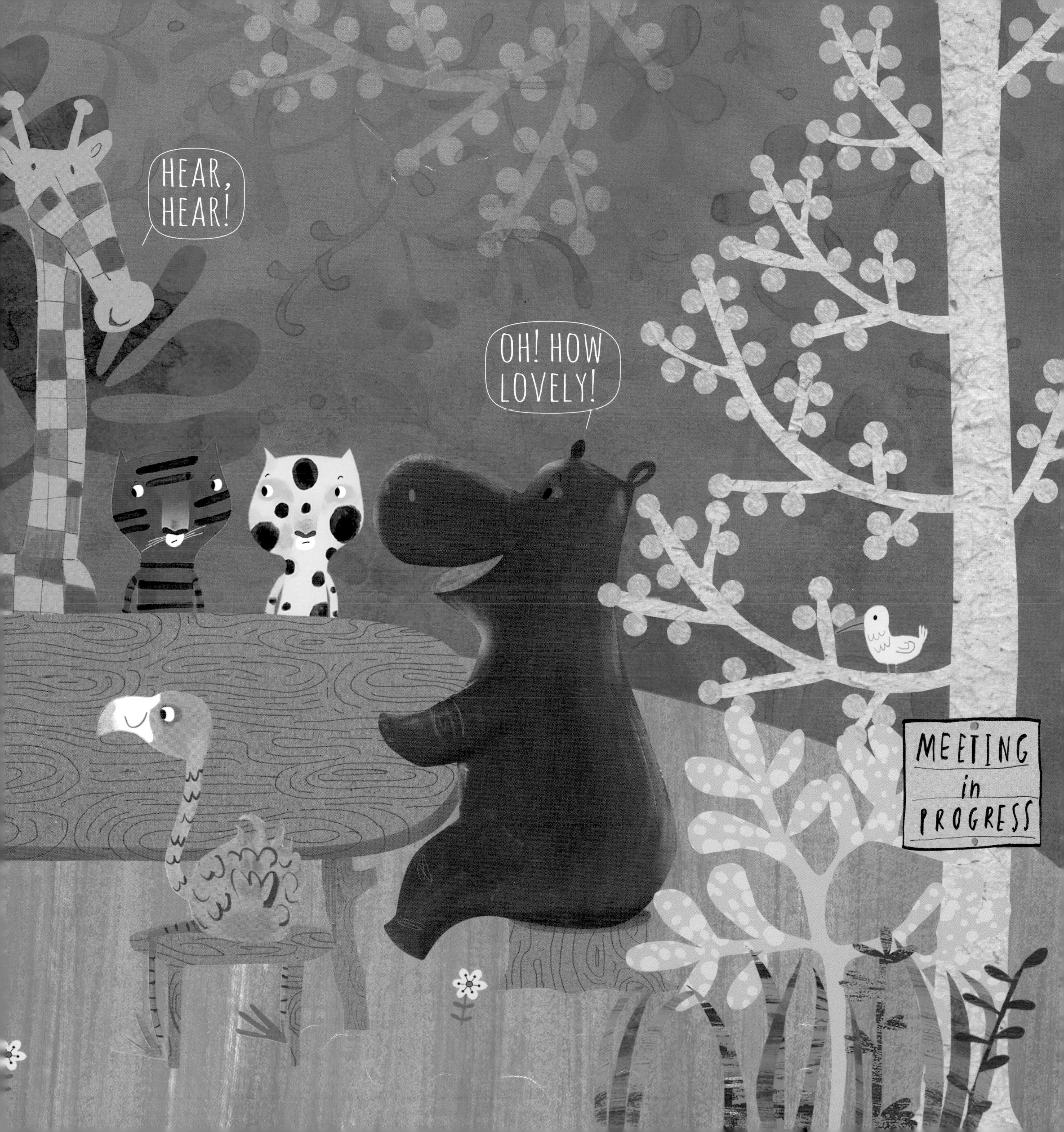
HEAR, HEAR!
OH! HOW LOVELY!
MEETING in PROGRESS

the JUN

A HUGE ROUND OF APPLAUSE FOR ALL THE CONTESTANTS!

the JUDGES

The following day...

PEACEFUL
JUNGLE
CONTEST

ALL WELCOME

WHEN: NOW
WHERE: HERE

Then the judges announced their favourites …

They liked Elephant's elegant suit.

WRINKLES ARE ALL THE RAGE!

And the nature expert's
green jacket.

WILD!

They were impressed with Tortoise's hardy shell.

A Bulletproof backpack!

And admired Giraffe's chequered coat.

CHEEKY CHECKS!

Hippopotamus was praised for her swanky swimsuit.

DRIP-DRY TOGS ARE VERY HIP!

Deep in the jungle,
all was at peace.

Well, sort of …

But they ADORED
Flamingo's fluffy,
pink plumage.

They loved Tiger's splendid stripes
and Leopard's fabulous spots.

SPOTS AND STRIPES
ARE ALWAYS STYLISH!

ESPECIALLY WHEN
THEY'RE TOGETHER.

And Peacock for his
multicoloured attire.

GROOVY!